THE LONGER WINTER

RSA
PRODUCTIONS

THE LONGER WINTER

There once was a family of birds named the Robinsons. They lived in the National Forest high in the trees, where several other bird families lived. They resided in a normal bird family neighborhood in a normal bird family town.

There was a dad named Henry, a mom named Mary, a teen brother named Christopher—Chris for short—a little sister named Nicole, and a baby brother named Danny.

One cold, windy fall day when the leaves were in their full fall colors, Henry was outside talking to the foreman from the Pelican Moving Company; a monkey named Mr. Bob.

"I like the fall moving special you have," Henry told Mr. Bob as he handed over his credit card. "It helps out a lot."

"Yes," Mr. Bob said, swiping the credit card on his tablet and giving Henry the receipt. "We've got a lot of takers on this special."

Mr. Bob saw two monkeys bringing bags out of the Robinson's house and packing them onto the backs of the pelicans.

"Make sure the strapping is tight," Mr. Bob yelled to the monkeys. "Watch the weight and make sure to put on an extra strap."

One of the monkeys saluted Mr. Bob and everyone got back to work.

Christopher was inside his room playing video games with his headset whereas his dad was working with Mr. Bob. His friends online were talking through their headsets about going to a beach party, but Chris was focused on the army mission game they were playing.

"Hey, Jimmy," Chris warned his friend, "watch your flank, I saw someone over there."

"I got it," Jimmy said.

"Hey, guys!" A girl's voice called out over the headsets. "I'm running low on ammo."

"I'll give you some of mine, Chrystal," Chris offered.

"A box of chocolate-covered grenades, too." Jimmy teased.

"Shut up, Jimmy," Chris said. He knew his friend was just teasing him for liking Chrystal and not telling her, but it still bugged him.

"Ok, everybody," David said. "Keep an eye out for snipers."

A second later, gunshots blasted from the game, with snipers firing at Chris and his friends, and their group firing back.

"Chris! Christopher!" Henry yelled from Chris's doorway. "Hey, stop playing that game and come help me board up the other side of the house."

Chris reached up and took one side of his headset off to hear his dad better. "Ok dad, let me finish this last life."

His dad folded his arms and said, "Ok, this shouldn't take long."

Chris died right away, and his dad laughed before heading out.

"Gotta go, guys," Chris said into his headset. "My dad wants me to help board up the house before we leave for winter."

"Christopher D. Robinson!" Chris heard his dad shout.

"Coming!" Chris hung up on his friends and ran out of his room. He tripped over one of Danny's baby toys and fell into a bucket of soapy water that his mom was using to mop the floors.

Bubbles streamed off of his head and baby Danny popped one of them and laughed.

His dad saw him, and he laughed as he helped Chris up. "Let's get to work."

Chris and his dad went outside on the porch and started boarding up the windows.

"Dad?" Chris said, wanting to ask his dad a question about girls that he'd been wondering for a while. "How did you know Mom was the one?"

"Well, Chris," his dad said. "Your mom was a cheerleader for the Blue Jays football team back in high school. I was the manager/water boy for the team and would mess up every time she came around."

Chris laughed at the image of his clumsy father and his cheerleader mother. He'd known they met in high school but had never asked for the full story.

"We both saw something in each other back then and that was it. Don't worry son, you will know when you know but if you ever need some advice on anything Chris, I'm here for you."

I know, Dad. Thanks. Chris said.

"No problem." They finished nailing boards on one of the windows and moved to another one, and Chris's dad changed the conversation. "Did your license come in the mail yet?"

"Not yet," Chris said nervously. "But it's being delivered today by UPS."

"Good, good," Dad said. "Because you know you can't travel without it."

"I know, I know," Chris said. "Online tracking says today."

Good, dad replied.

Chris faked a smile, but he felt guilty for not telling his dad the truth. He'd skipped all of his flying lessons to play video game tournaments at the mall's video shop.

To distract himself, he took a closer look at the electric pulley system with a basket attachment his dad had designed. "What do you use the pulley for mostly?" he asked.

"Well," his dad said "I use it to get my tools up high into the trees to work on the electric grid, and to go down just to the edge of the fog below. I try not to ever use it to go below the fog unless it's an emergency."

Chris looked over the side of the porch and saw the fog down below the lowest branches. "What's down there?"

His dad's face turned serious. "Don't ever go down there! That's not a place for us."

"Why? What's down there below the fog?"

"Evil forces loom down there," his dad said, voice quiet, almost as though he was afraid of being heard. "Long, slimy creatures with big fangs that eat everything in sight, including birds."

"Have you ever been down there?"

"NO! But we have had neighbors venture down there, never to return; the elder council has written stories about the Down Below."

Chris didn't ask his father any more questions about the fog or what was below it. His dad was an electrical engineer and a smart guy. If he was afraid of the Down Below, Chris figured he was right to be.

When they were finished with the house, they went back inside and sat around the dinner table as a family to eat.

"Dad, Mom, I was wondering if it would be ok if I travel south on my own this year?" he asked.

Both of his parents stopped eating.

"Absolutely not," his dad said. "Why would you want to do that?"

"You're too young," his mom said.

"He just wants to spend some time with Chrystal," Nicole chimed in.

"Shut up!" Chris snapped.

"Okay, you two," their mom said. "no fighting at the table."

"I'm almost 15," Chris argued. "Lots of birds travel on their own at 15."

"Lots don't have us as parents," his mom said.

"Come on," Chris pleaded, seeing all of his plans to stop with his friends in Orlando go up in smoke.

"Why do you want to travel alone?" his dad asked again.

"A couple of my friends are meeting up in Orlando this year," Chris admitted. "It's a kinda spring break in the fall, and I really want to go with them."

"I don't know if that's a good idea," his dad said, though he didn't sound as sure as he had before.

His mom looked over at his dad with a sharp look in her eyes. "Are you really considering this?" she asked.

"Well, he is coming of age, Mary."

"And I do all my chores," Chris said. "I have good grades, I take care of my brother and sister, and I'm responsible; it will be safe.

I'm going with some of my other friends, so you could call their parents to check and work together on this. Please?" He gave his parents his most beseeching look, the one he'd been using since he was a little chick asking for extra dessert after dinner.

"I don't know," his mom said uncertainly.

"Your mom and I will talk about it. We'll let you know later."

"Ok," Chris said with a smile.

Later that night, Henry and Mary were alone in their bedroom. Henry was sitting back in bed reading a book, his glasses perched high on his beak. Mary sat at her make-up table, examining herself in the mirror.

"So," Mary said, "do you think it would be a good idea if he goes by himself?"

"Well, he did hit on some really good points of why we should let him," Henry said.

"I guess I agree. He is growing up," Mary said.

"He is," Henry replied.

Mary let out a sigh. "Then we let him fly on his own," she said.

She heard the familiar sound of her oldest son's feet coming down the hall. "Chris, come in here for a minute," she called.

He appeared quickly in their bedroom.

"Dad and I talked it over and decided to let you do this. You can fly down on your own with your friends."

Chris jumped up and down in excitement, his wings flapping by his sides.

"Thanks, Mom and Dad, I won't let you down!"

"You better not," his dad warned.

The next day, the rest of Chris's family was ready to leave. His parents were all loaded up, all the baggage they needed to bring strapped to his dad's back; the baby and Chris's little sister Nicole, who wore a pink backpack, secure on his mom's back.

They had a few words to say to him before leaving, though. "Make sure to lock the house up before you leave, and be careful traveling," his dad advised.

"And tell me again exactly what you are doing," his mom demanded.

"I'm leaving in three hours," Chris told her. "I'm meeting up with my friends, flying down to Orlando for two days, and then meeting you guys in Miami."

"Wait, do you know how to fly?" his mom asked. "I haven't seen you fly yet; did you finish your flying exams?"

Chris nodded enthusiastically. "Don't worry, I have it all under control. I'm great at flying. I'm an ace!"

"Oh, ok," his mom said.

"I'm trusting in you to do what you're supposed to do," Chris's dad told him seriously.

"I will. It's ok, Dad. Have fun. I'll be there in a couple of days."

Birds from neighboring houses were taking off, a whole flock of them, and Chris's parents flew up to join them on the journey south.

Three hours later, Chris was on the porch talking on his cell phone with one of his friends, finalizing their plans.

"Chris, are you going to meet up with us or what? We're flying off if you're here or not in like 30 minutes," Jimmy said.

"I'll be there, I'll be there," Chris replied and hung up his cell phone. He put it in his pocket. Following his father's directions on locking everything up, he stood on the porch, ready to fly off. "Ok, you can do this," he said to himself. "Here we go!"

He backed up a bit to give himself a running start, then ran off the porch and started to fly.

It felt good to have the air under his wings. "Oh, this is easy," Chris said, surprised.

Comfortable, he paused the flapping of his wings and dropped quickly down toward and through the fog below.

"No, no, no," he said. He flapped his wings quickly again in panic, trying to fly again, but he couldn't. He hit the ground hard.

He struggled to sit up, dazed, and confused about what had just happened. It was dark down here, under the fog. He sees the light from the cell phone that fell out of his pocket during the fall to the ground, and he snatched it up to call for help. The "no service" message flashing on the screen was nearly enough to make him throw the useless phone, but he put it back in his pocket just in case.

He looked around, and through the fog he could see glowing eyes.

He began to shake.

Slowly, three figures emerged from the fog. A rabbit, a squirrel, and a deer, he thought. He'd seen squirrels before, up in the trees, but the other two he recognized only from stories.

"Hello?" Chris said hesitantly.

"Hello," the rabbit answered. "My name is Jack. This is Billy," he said with a nod of his head toward the squirrel, "and Emily."

Chris began to breathe a little easier. His dad had said everything under the fog wanted to eat him, but these three didn't seem too dangerous.

"What are you doing down here?" Jack asked.

"I slipped?" Chris suggested.

Jack and the others looked at him sideways, like they didn't quite believe him. "But you're a bird," Billy said. "Birds don't come down here"

"I know," Chris said defensively, irritated with the squirrel. "I know. I can't fly. Are you happy now?"

"Can't fly?" Billy asked. "Well, that doesn't make any sense. All the birds I've seen can fly."

"I didn't go to flying class. I kinda skipped and played video games."

"Wow," Emily said. "A bird that can't fly. Who would have ever thought?"

Chris stood up and dusted himself off. "I know, I know."

"Ok, let's go," Jack said.

"Where are you guys going?" Chris asked, not wanting to be left alone.

"The river. The twins are at it again" Jack said.

"The twins?" Chris replied.

"Yea," Billy said. "It's a couple of beavers that go at it when they're building stuff." He laughed. "You'll see."

The others started to leave and head toward the river, but Chris hesitated, looking back up the tree to his house, lingering for a bit.

"Come on," Emily said.

At the river, Chris saw the beavers the others had referred to as the twins; arguing while working on building a bridge.

Chris leaned over and whispered to Emily, "Why are they called twins when there's three of them?"

"Don't ask," Emily told him.

"This is off!" the beaver who seemed to be in charge said. "Did you even look at the blueprints?"

"Dude, Al, we're beavers! Really?" the other beaver argued.

"Hey, guys," Billy said to the beavers. "I guess I won't ask how the project is coming, but we have a guest."

"He's from the treetops," Emily added.

"Really?" the lead beaver asked. "What are you doing down here? Your kind NEVER travels down here."

"Well, it's a long story," Chris said sadly.

"And a long fall," Jack added, laughing.

The beavers stared at the four of them like they didn't get it. They didn't wait long, though, before the lead beaver barked at the other two, "Ok, back to work."

"Alright, come on guys," Billy said. "Let's leave them to work and head to the festival."

"What's that?" Chris asked.

"It's a big outdoor get-together, like a street fair," Emily told him.

"Yea, with lots of great food," Billy added.

Jack hopped in front of the beavers. "Ok fellas, we'll check back with you later. Do you want us to bring you some food back?"

"No," Al said. "That's OK, we're coming over there shortly."

"But save me an elephant ear or two," a different beaver asked.

The leader looked at his twin—triplet? —sharply. "Really, Adam, an elephant ear? A beaver eating an elephant ear?"

"Yea, what's wrong with that?" Adam asked.

"Can't you see the oxymoron in that?" Al replied.

"You're a moron," Adam said.

The two started wrestling and fell off the log they were standing on with a splash into the water.

"We'll see you later!" Jack called cheerily before hopping off into the woods, his friends and Chris following behind him.

They ran into other animals on the way, the first one a snake.

"It's a snake!" Chris said in fear, remembering his dad warning him of the long, slimy creatures with fangs that were waiting to eat him beneath the fog.

The snake jumped, looking around as though scared of Chris's warning.

"That's just Sammy," Jack reassured him.

Chris looked closer at the snake, unsure, but Sammy didn't look that scary. He wore big glasses and a multicolored hat, accompanied by a beautiful butterfly.

"Where are you guys headed?" the butterfly asked, her voice whisper-soft, like her paper-thin wings.

"I bet they're going to the fair," Sammy said.

"Yup, we are," Emily confirmed. She glanced over at Chris, who looked overwhelmed. "Chris, this is Mya," she said, introducing the butterfly. "You've met Sammy. They're our friends."

Chris nodded.

"Are you guys going to the fair?" Emily asked Sammy and Mya.

"Yea, we are, but you better watch out for the Braxton Boys."

"Who are the Braxton Boys?" Chris asked, not sure how much more his brain could take.

Mya flew over and landed delicately in front of Chris. "The Braxton Boys are three of the meanest wolves you'll ever meet," she said, the harsh warning sounding strange coming from her soft, wispy voice. "Kano, Jake, and Markus. If you ever see them, you better run, because otherwise, you'll become dinner."

"Yea, they are not good," Billy confirmed.

"Oh!" Chris gulped audibly.

All of a sudden, a hedgehog popped up out of the ground. "Yea, yea they are NOT good!"

Chris jumped back, heart pounding at the sight of the spiky creature.

"Pete, are you eavesdropping again?" Mya chided.

"Nope, nope," Pete responded, his words almost tripping over each other in their speed. "Wouldn't do that, not me, nope."

Everyone chuckled a bit and continued to the fair. Jack hopped along, Emily walking sedately beside him. Billy moved hurriedly, his path zigzagging, scurrying partway up the side of trees at random before joining them back on the ground. Pete kept up with a quick pitter-patter of little feet, with Sammy slithering slowly behind, and Mya gliding along almost lazily on her thin wings.

Chris struggled to keep up, his claws awkward on the forest floor as he alternately walked and hopped along.

Upon a nearby hill, three wolves were looking down into the trees. The leader, Kano, licked his lips.

"Looks like dinner is gonna be good tonight," he said to his younger brothers. "Right, Jake?"

Jake jumped and twitched, "Yea, yea, dinner's gonna be good tonight."

"I'm with that," the third brother, Markus, added.

They started down the hill toward the other animals, tracking them for a later ambush.

Back in the woods, Chris and his friends were nearing the edge, where a clearing with grass and flowers awaited them. Chris had found the solution to keeping up with the gang by riding on Emily's back, and Mya rode on Emily's head.

"So let me get this straight," Mya said. "You can't fly? You are a bird, right?"

"I know, I know. I skipped out on those lessons," he said guiltily.

"Lessons? Don't all birds just know how to fly naturally?"

"Not us," Chris said. "It takes a lot of work to learn to get your balance and fly."

"Wow," Mya said.

"Think about it, I'm not like you," Chris said. "You start as one thing and turn into another. You couldn't fly before, and now you can. But even after you were reborn, it still took you a minute to get it, right?"

"How do you know all that?" Mya asked.

"I learned it in school," Chris said. "I didn't skip all my lessons."

"That's good," Mya said. "But you're older than a minute. Why'd it take you so long to learn?"

"You have a point," Chris said.

"Don't worry," Mya assured him in her whisper. "You'll get there."

The surrounding animals chimed in with their assurances for the grounded robin. At the edge of the forest, blocking the group from the clearing, were fallen trees. They were piled so high that even Emily couldn't see over them.

Billy climbed up to the top of the fallen trees with ease, and Pete went underground to pop up on the other side. Emily with Mya and Chris on her back, Jack and Sammy all headed left to go around the pile of trees, until Billy and Pete appeared back on their side of the trees.

"The Braxton Boys are on the other side!" Billy cried. "Run!"

The group turned to start running back the way they'd come, but the Braxton Boys must have heard them.

"Let's go, boys," Kano's deep, growly voice came from the other side of the tree trunks.

Everyone ran along, Emily in the front, Chris holding tight to her fur with his feet. Jack was just as fast, each hop sending him flying further down the clearing. The others were close behind, but when Chris turned, he saw that the Braxton Boys had made it around the logs and were now on their side of the obstacle.

"Get 'em!" Kano howled.

They made it to the river much faster than Chris had thought possible, jumping in, free-falling down into the churning water just before the wolves could get to them.

Kano's teeth snapped shut right behind Emily's rear leg, and his momentum carried him a bit over the edge before his brothers grabbed him and pulled him back.

"Come on," Kano said. "We'll get them downstream."

The wolves started making their way back into the tree line and downriver to a place where the riverbank wasn't so steep.

Down in the river, the group made it to a floating, flat piece of wood that they could all climb on. Chris, who was a stranger to the river, found himself nearly getting swept off Emily's back by the strong currents. He felt a tug at his pocket and looked down to see his cellphone slip out, pulled by the force of the river. He grabbed for it, but it was just out of reach. He watched helplessly as it swirled away downstream before he gave up and hopped up onto Emily's head, then onto the piece of wood.

The beavers must have seen them on their way to the fair. They were walking in a row, Al in the lead, when they looked down at the river and noticed the group. He stopped his brothers and they all jumped into action, hurrying to get downstream of the group and moving trees to help direct them to the right side of the river.

The group jumped off their makeshift float and made it to the other side of the river, thankful for the beavers' help and shaking from their close call with the Braxton Boys.

As they started walking through the woods again, once more headed toward the fall fair, the last time many of the animals in the forest would see each other before hibernating for the long winter, the Braxton Boys found a fallen tree spanning across the river. Hunting was harder in the winter, and they were looking forward to a good dinner on a fair day. While the rest of the animals made it to the safety of the fair, the Braxton Boys watched from the edge of the forest, drooling from the thought of eating them all for dinner.

Later that afternoon, Chris and his group of friends were forced to say goodbye to the other animals at the fair. Chris's new friends had decided not to hibernate and help Chris survive the winter.

"It's going to be fun to see the place turn to a winter wonderland, but we're gonna need a lot of food to make it through the winter until spring," Jack said.

"I don't need too much," Sammy said. "But I can help you find some."

"I'm pretty good at building things and hiding nuts in them," Billy offered.

"We should be fine," Pete said.

Chris had a worried look on his face, and Emily looked at him with empathy. "Don't worry, we will be fine." Emily turned to address the rest of the group. "How about finding a cave?" she suggested. "There are some really good ones near the big hill. It's kinda heated from the mountain."

Everyone seemed to agree with Emily's proposal.

"Great idea," Pete and Mya said.

"This will be the first time I get to see snow," Chris said, growing excited about the prospect.

"You've never seen snow before?" Jack asked.

"He's a bird," Emily said. "They go south for the winter."

"I only read about it in books; this is gonna be fun," Chris said.

The group found a cave big enough for them all to fit and built a covered porch area in front of it so they would be able to stand and see the winter snow without it falling on their heads.

They all started gathering surplus food for the winter, excited and happy for the adventure to come.

They couldn't know that this would be one of the worst winters to come along in a long time. When the rain started, they gathered inside and watched it, happy that they were dry and together.

As they stood huddled at the front door of the cave, they heard a deep voice from behind them.

"What are we looking at?" the voice asked.

Everyone turned to look at each other. "Who said that?" they asked.

"I want to see," the deep voice said. "Move aside."

Without looking back to see who had spoken this time, they all started running out of the cave into the rain. Once they'd gained what they thought of was a safe distance, they looked back to see a small bear emerge from the cave.

"You guys woke me up," he accused.

"What are you doing here?" Jack demanded.

"I live here. I was sleeping. Hibernating?" the bear said.

"Where are your parents?" Emily asked because the bear didn't look big enough to be on his own, even if his voice was deep.

"They left a while ago and never came back," the bear said sadly.

"That's sad," Billy said, looking around for any other bears. "You think they may come back?"

"Maybe one day, I don't know. I thought I could just go to sleep, and they would be here when I woke up."

"Sorry we woke you," Pete said.

"That's OK," the bear said. "I was getting lonely anyway." he paused. "My name is Bobby," another pause. "I'm really hungry; you guys have any food?"

As if in answer, the beavers showed up, pulling behind them a board loaded with fish to eat for the winter. Everyone turned to look at the bounty.

"Yes!!" Bobby cheered. "I love fish."

That night inside the cave, they sat around the fire Bobby had built, cooking their fish on sticks the beavers had cut.

"How do you know how to do that?" Billy asked the bear.

"Just before my dad left to get food for the winter, my parents both taught me how to do this," Bobby said, expertly turning his stick so that the fish cooked on both sides as his parents had taught him. "They started to teach me to fish also, but they didn't get a chance to finish."

"You said just before your dad left?" Jack asked. "How about your mom?"

"About a day after dad left, me and my mom were here in the cave talking when we heard a strange noise from outside. It was a growling sound, and she told me to stay here inside while she looked around outside. I heard talking—it was a pack of wolves."

"The Braxton Boys!" Al said.

"They wanted me, but my mom said no, and as they tried to come in, Mom fought them off and they all tried to attack her. I was really scared. She shouted for me to hide and fought with them and chased them back into the woods. They must have gotten her. I heard her make this sound I will never forget, and then there was silence.

I stayed inside and cried, waiting for her to return, but she never did, so I just fell asleep, and then I heard you guys."

"Wow, I'm so sorry that happened to you," Chris said.

"Thanks," Bobby replied.

Outside the rain turned to snow, and they were all surprised and excited by the fat white flakes. Chris was shocked, and he got up from the fire to get a closer look.

"This is snow?" he asked. "Does it hurt?"

"No! It's fun," Billy said.

The twins started laughing and running around. "Yea, it's great!"

"Yea, it's," a snowball hit Sammy in the back of the head "great," he finished. Snow now covered his multi-colored hat and splattered across his glasses.

One of the beavers, Aiden, threw another snowball at Sammy, laughing as others joined in the snowball fight.

Sammy teamed up with Chris, rolling the balls with his tail so that Chris could throw them.

On the hill, unseen by the laughing group, the Braxton Brothers watched hungrily

It snowed all night, but the fire in the cave kept the group warm as they slept. In the morning, Jack sat up with a yawn. "Boy, do I feel good. I haven't slept that good in a long time," he said.

"Yea," Pete agreed. "That was pretty good."

Jack pulled a toothbrush out of his pocket and headed in the direction that would take him outside of the cave. With his eyes only half-open, he didn't see the mountain of snow until he stepped in it, up to his ears.

He shouted and the twins came out, walking carefully on the snow, so as not to fall through themselves.

Alex grabbed Jack by the ears and pulled; once the rabbit was out, he began spitting out snow.

"You need to watch your step there, chief," Alex said.

"Thanks," Jack said, wide-awake after the close call.

"I've seen this before when I was a fawn," Emily said. "It's just the beginning. We need to take shelter and get ready. See those clouds up there?" They all looked up at the dark, black clouds building in the morning sky. "It's coming." The group separates into pairs and walks into the woods to gather supplies.

"Em, why are you here with us?" Chris asked Emily as he sat perched on her back, keeping an eye out for more food as she walked through the woods. "Don't you have a family to be with?" The snow had turned to rain, and Chris resigned himself to wet feathers for the rest of the day.

"Actually, I don't. My parents were killed by hunters last spring. I've been on my own ever since."

"Wow, did you see it happen?" he asked.

Emily nodded. "I did. I was back in the tree line when it happened, but there wasn't anything I could do."

Emily took a few steps through the snow that was quickly turning to slush. Without warning, the ground gave out beneath her feet and she fell into a deep hunter's trap. She tried to climb out the side of the hole, but the dirt had turned to mud from the rain and her hooves kept slipping.

The rain changed from a drizzle to a downpour, causing the water to fill up the hole faster and faster.

"What are we gonna do?" Chris asked in a panic. He jumped from Emily's back to her head, trying to see out of the hole.

"It's up to you to get help," Emily said. "I can't get out."

Chris jumped and flapped his wings vigorously but fell back down. He tried again and again to fly, finally letting out a scream of frustration as he once more fell back into the hole.

"I'm sorry," Chris said, nearly in tears.

"That's OK," Emily said. "You tried." Her voice was so full of understanding. "Maybe it's just my time."

Chris shook his head, upset with himself that because of him, Emily was stuck in this hole with no way to get out. He tried again to fly, flapping his wings harder and harder, and then he was flying!

He flew up out of the hole and looked back at Emily, who seemed as surprised as he was.

"Go, Chris, go!" she yelled.

"I'll be back; I'll get help. Hold on!"

"Hurry," Emily said quietly as she looked around at her bleak situation. Soon after she heard a familiar sound and looked up to see the glowing eyes of the Braxton Boys watching her.

"We finally get to have a venison dinner," Jake said.

"Yes, yes, about time," Markus chimed.

Chris flew as hard as he could through the trees and branches. The storm was getting worse, with branches breaking off and leaves blowing everywhere. He dodged leaves and branches when suddenly a branch fell right in front of him. He had no room to dodge, and it hit him, sending him spiraling to the ground.

When Chris woke up the rain was still falling, the wind still blowing through the trees. He wasn't sure how long he had been unconscious, but he knew he couldn't fail Emily. He might already be too late, she might have already drowned, but he had to get help no matter what; he started to fly again.

He began yelling as soon as he was in sight of the cave.

"Everyone, hey, everybody! Emily needs help!"

He flew right into the cave, surprising everyone at his newfound ability. His quick words cut through any congratulations, however. "Emily needs help! She fell in a hole and it's filling up with water. She'll drown if we don't hurry! Hurry!"

Emily did her best to stay away from the edges of the hole, where the Braxton Boys snapped hungrily at her. She was getting tired, trying to keep her head above water, and now she couldn't even try to get herself out anymore.

Kano snapped at her again, but this time he reached out too far. He fell in the hole, splashing Emily with cold, muddy water.

Jake and Markus egged their brother on. Emily flailed her legs, her tiny hooves kicking out at Kano while he bit at her.

"Get her!" Jake yelled.

"Right, left," Markus instructed.

"Bring her up here!"

Chris could hear the Braxton Boys as he flew back to the hole, his friends' right behind him. The rain was coming down in sheets, lightning flashing, as the two groups stared at each other and Emily and Kano, still thrashing in the water, both struggling not to drown.

The Braxton Boys growled at Chris and his friends' arrival.

"Look, we both know this is an awkward situation," Markus said. "But we need each other if we're going to help them."

"What are you talking about?" Jake snapped. "We need to eat them, not help them!"

"No," Markus said. "We'll work together and figure the rest out later!"

"Deal!" Bobby said before they could argue more. "Emily needs help NOW!" He walked over to the hole, careful not to fall in, and saw both Emily and Kano struggling to breathe. "Get some tree vines!" he shouted.

Both groups worked together to get the tree vines and make a pulley to pull them out. Emily grabbed the vines with her mouth and Kano climbed on her back. Slowly, Emily was able to walk up the side of the hole with the help of her friends pulling her and Kano up, with Bobby as the anchor.

When they finally reached the top of the hole, both Emily and Kano collapsed on the ground, breathing heavily.

Jake lunged at Emily, trying to bite her, but Kano tackled his brother just before he got a taste.

"What are you doing?" Jake asked as they wrestled on the wet ground. "I had her!"

"NO! We're not doing this now," Kano shouted.

"What, you're turning soft on me?"

"NO!" Kano repeated. "I said not NOW."

Jake smirked. "OK, Kano. Whatever you say." He shook his head and slowly headed into the woods.

"Wait, Jake!" Markus called. "Kano!"

23

"He'll be OK," Kano promised.

Markus gave Kano a regretful look and ran to catch up with Jake. "Hey, wait up" he called.

Kano looked at the group around him, then at Emily who gave him a grateful smile.

"Thanks, I know that was hard," Emily said.

"Don't thank me yet," Kano replied.

"Well, thank you for now," she said.

Kano started to walk after his brothers. He looked back once at Emily and the rest of the group, then huffed and ran off into the woods.

A violent shock of lightning lit the air around them, followed by thunder loud enough to shake the trees. The storm was getting worse.

"Let's get back to the cave!" Jack shouted over the noise.

The Braxton Boys made it back to their campsite and Jake asked Kano, "What's wrong with you? If you don't have the heart to lead anymore; maybe you should step aside and let a real leader lead"

Jake scowled at Kano like he was ready to attack him. Markus looked nervous, not knowing what was about to happen.

He tried to calm the situation. "Come on, fellas, we can work this out," Markus said.

Jake and Kano circled as if they are about to attack each other, and as they lunged for each other, a bolt of lightning flashed as their fight ensued.

Both of them got in some good bites and scratches when Jake slipped and fell backward into a tree trunk. A large branch fell on him as the storm continued, injuring him.

Kano looked at his brother and instantly regretted the fight. He and Markus both ran over to help remove the tree branch that fell on Jake and found him only semi-conscious.

The other group traveled back to the cave where it was dry and still warm because of the fire, they had left burning. Emily sat closest to the fire warming herself after her long time trapped in the cold, wet hole. The wind howled outside, competing with the heavy rain for noise.

The group heard what must have been a large tree falling, followed by a howl that wasn't the wind.

It was a pained cry.

Emily got up and approached the pile of debris they'd placed near the door to block more of the rain and wind out. She saw Kano coming toward the cave, helping Jake walk with an arm slung over his shoulder. Markus walked beside them.

Emily caught Kano's eyes, and Kano paused for a second. But Emily knew they needed shelter and food desperately, and she began clearing the debris out of the entrance before Kano had to ask.

"Come on," Emily said, knowing she was taking a risk letting them in. She led them toward the fire, and the boys sat around it gratefully. The twins and Chris helped pile blankets on the brothers, and when Markus sneezed, Jack handed him a cup of hot soup.

"Thanks," Markus said, giving the rabbit a small smile.

Jack laughed, then Sammy and Pete joined in. Markus and Kano laughed, too, until everyone but Jake was laughing.

Markus elbowed his brother, and Jake began smiling and laughing under his breath, too.

Green spring grass began to poke out of the previously cold ground, and the twins came out of a deep hole underground. Alex had his hard hat on, but the other two wore only robes and carried cups of coffee.

"Get to work," Alex scolded them.

"I'm going back to bed," Adam and Aiden said in unison as they walked back underground.

Alcx followed after them. "Come on, fellas. We have a lot of work to do."

A few minutes later, the twins returned. It was spring now, and once Aiden and Adam took a moment to wake up, they were happy to enjoy the warm spring sunshine instead of the inside of their holes.

Chris was happy that it was spring, too. The winter with his friends had been great. The creatures that lived below the fog weren't horrible monsters after all—they were just like him.

And he could fly now, too! He looked up at the sky and saw that the birds were returning home after their long winter in Florida.

"Well, guys, I think I have to go," Chris told his friends.

"Why?" Pete asked.

"I think I need to be up there when my parents get back to explain why I didn't meet them in Miami."

"We understand," Jack and Emily said together.

"But don't be a stranger," Jack added. "You have friends down here now."

"I know," Chris replied.

Everyone came up to Chris and hugged him. "I won't say goodbye," Chris said. "Just 'I'll see you later.'"

They all smiled at him, and he took off, flying up to his house. He saw that his family had just returned, with his dad pulling the boards off the front door and opening it.

"It's good to be back," he heard his dad say with sadness in his voice. Chris realized that all of this time, his parents wouldn't have known what happened to him. They probably thought he was dead.

He flapped his wings faster and landed before his family in a rush. The shock and surprise on his family's face were quickly replaced by happy smiles and tears.

Everyone rushed to him, grabbing and hugging, his mother clinging to him as though she never wanted to let go.

"What happened? Where were you?" everyone asked at the same time, giving Chris no time to answer.

"We thought you were dead," his mother said tearfully.

She gave Nicole and Danny a grateful look and the kids ran inside the house. Chris's parents stayed behind to speak to him about why he hadn't met up with them in Miami.

"I'm sorry," Chris said as he confessed skipping his flying lessons and falling through the fog because he didn't know how to fly.

They listened as he explained everything that had happened to him, from meeting his friends to Emily almost drowning, to helping the Braxton Brothers during the storm and the great time he'd had with his friends all winter.

"You had us worried," his dad said.

"I'm just glad you're OK," his mom added.

Chris's mom headed inside, and Chris stayed out with his dad and helped him take down the boards from the windows. He went over to the pulley and looked over. His friends were down in the basket below.

"Dad, I have someone for you to meet," he said, pushing the button that would bring the basket up.

"What are you doing?" his dad asked.

"You'll see," Chris replied.

When the pulley reached the top, everyone got out slowly. Chris's family emerged from the house, and the birds and forest animals regarded each other apprehensively.

Chris introduced the two groups to each other. "Dad, Mom, these are my friends I told you about.

Jack stepped forward a little nervously. "Nice to meet you, Mr. and Mrs. Robinson." He handed Chris's mom a bouquet of multicolored spring flowers he'd picked below.

Chris's mom accepted them graciously. "Why don't you all come inside? I have lunch ready."

Everyone filed inside, talking excitedly as they got to know each other over lunch on a late spring afternoon.

The End.

THE LONGER WINTER

Writer & Creator: T. Bradley

Editor: Jordyn McGinnity

Illustrator: Max Alnutt

Readers: Diane Tarver / Nicole Harris-Glass / Courtney Peterson / Joseph Andolina / Vicky Gibson / Nancy Lloyd / Vanessa Lemus / Lorraine Urbina / Ricky Santiago / Emma Anderson / Jyoti Sharma / Susan Cardona / Cassie Schmierer / Sharon Baker / Scott Douglas /Constance Parbon / Jeannie Allen / Elissa Monk / Stacy Chambless/ Rosetta Bradley / Kevin Bradley/ Sharon Baker/ Rose Andolina.

Producer: Stephanie Bradley

First Edition

www.thelongerwinter.com

Publishing & Distribution by:

RSA Productions
P.O. Box 12246
Mill Creek, WA 98082

ISBN 978-1-09839-834-7
thelongerwinter@gmail.com

The Robinsons

Chris   Henry   Mary   Nicole   Danny

Coming Next
The Longer Spring / The Longer Summer / The Longer Fall

"THE LONGER SERIES"

THE LONGER WINTER

The Robinsons

Chris   Henry   Mary   Nicole   Danny

©®